Just Right

For Adrian
B.B.

To my niece Gracie, with love
R.B

First published 2011 by Nosy Crow Ltd
The Crow's Nest, 10a Lant Street
London SE1 1QR
www.nosycrow.com

This edition published 2011

ISBN 978 0 85763 083 4

Nosy Crow and associated logos are trademark
and or registered trademarks of Nosy Crow Ltd.

Text copyright © Birdie Black 2011
Illustration copyright © Rosalind Beardshaw 2011

The right of Birdie Black to be identified as the author
and Rosalind Beardshaw as the illustrator of this work has been asserted.

A CIP catalogue record for this book is available from the British Library.

Printed in Singapore

10 9 8 7 6 5 4 3 2 1

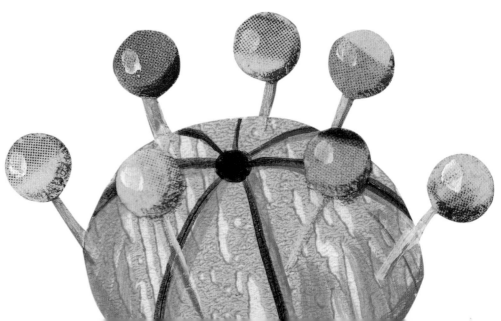

Just Right

Birdie Black

Illustrated by

Rosalind Beardshaw

nosy crow

It was Christmas Eve, and snow was falling as the king strolled round the market. What should he see but a huge roll of beautiful bright red cloth!

"Oooh!" he said. "That cloth is so red and soft and Christmassy! It would be just right for a grand cloak for the princess!" And so he bought it and took it back to his castle.

In the castle, the king's sewing maids snipped and they sewed and they snipped and they sewed and, by lunchtime, they had made a beautiful long cloak for the princess.
The king was delighted.

He wrapped it up in golden paper and silver ribbon.
"What shall we do with the scraps?"
one of the sewing maids asked.
"Oh, just bundle them up and put them outside
the back door," said the king.

Jenny the castle kitchen-maid had finished work for
the day. What should she see on her way home but
a big bundle of beautiful bright red scraps?
"Oooh!" she said. "That cloth is so red and soft
and Christmassy! It would be just right
to make a jacket for my ma!"

When Jenny got home,
she snipped and she sewed and
she snipped and she sewed and . . .

. . . by tea-time, she'd made
a smart red jacket
for her ma.

She was very happy, and she wrapped it up in red paper with a green ribbon.

Then she bundled up the little scraps and put them outside the back door so her ma wouldn't see them.

Bertie Badger trotted past Jenny's house.
What should he see but a little bundle of beautiful
bright red scraps?
"Oooh!" he said. "That cloth is so red and soft and
Christmassy! It would be just right to make a hat for my pa!"

When Bertie got home,
he snipped and he sewed

and he snipped
and he sewed and . . .

by the time the clock
was striking six . . .

Then he bundled up the tiny scraps and put them outside the back door.

He smiled as he wrapped it up in some brown paper and tied it with string.

. . . he'd made a smart red hat for his pa.

Samuel Squirrel bounded past
Bertie's house. Suddenly, he stopped.
What should he see but a tiny bundle of
beautiful bright red scraps?
"Oooh!" he said. "That cloth is so red and
soft and Christmassy! It would be just right
to make a pair of gloves for my wife!"

When Samuel got home, he snipped and
he sewed and he snipped and
he sewed and . . .

by the time the moon was
rising, he'd made a beautiful
pair of gloves for his wife.

He wrapped them in a leaf,
and tied it with a piece
of dried grass.

"It's just as well I've made her something
to keep her hands warm," he said.
"This winter wind is so chilly!"
A gust picked up the tiny scrap of red cloth that
was left over and blew it out of his window,
where it fluttered to the snowy ground.

It was nearly midnight when Milly Mouse
plodded past Samuel's house.
She was tired and cold, and the snow was falling on her
ears and whiskers. She had been looking for a nut to give
to little Billy for Christmas, but she couldn't find one.

As she passed the bottom of Samuel's tree,
she saw something red sticking out of the snow.

What could it be?

It was the tiny scrap of cloth!
"Oooh!" she said. "That cloth is so soft and
red and Christmassy. It would be just right
to make a scarf for my Billy!"

Billy was asleep when Milly got
home. She snipped
and she sewed and . . .

she snipped and she sewed
and, by the time the candle had
burnt down, she'd made a
cosy scarf for Billy.

She didn't have anything to wrap it in, but she folded it carefully
and put it under her tiny sprig of Christmas tree.

And on Christmas morning,
the princess opened her
huge gold present.

And Jenny's ma opened her
big red present.

And Bertie's pa opened his small brown-paper present.

And Samuel's wife unwrapped her leaf.

And Milly gave little Billy his scarf.

Each present was so soft and red and Christmassy, and felt just right . . .

. . . just how Christmas should feel.

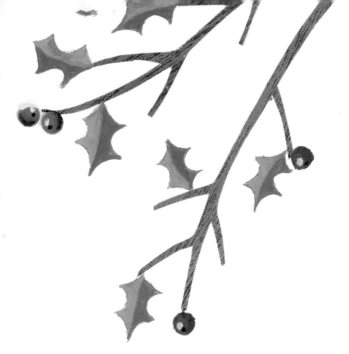